A VINEYARD VALENTINE

A VINEYARD
VALENTINE

NINA BOCCI

A VINEYARD VALENTINE
Published initially as an audio original with Audible
ISBN: 978-1-7375481-3-3

I

Chapter One

"Rise and shine, Eloisa! Are you alive?"

I smiled at the sound of my best friend's voice, turning my head to push my face into the comfort of my soft pillow only to be met with a hard table and a stack of papers stuck to my face. I realized I wasn't tucked under my warm homemade quilt or nestled on my fluffy queen- sized bed. I was chilled to the bone with a crick in my neck after falling asleep on my desk.

Again. "This is the worst."

"Ello, I know you're up there, I brought coffee!" she called using my childhood nickname.

"It can't be morning yet," I shouted down to the first floor of the barn. I only closed my eyes for a second.

"We have a meeting in forty-five minutes!"

Last night, I was working on a new label design for Giordano Cellars, my family's winery.

One of the first things I did when I took over after my father's retirement was decide we needed to rebrand and that label mock-up was now stuck to my cheek. Our original label was very ornate, yet a bit out of date – at least in my opinion. My new design was sleek, modern but still classic. Classical contemporary was how I was hoping to reinvent the entire company, hoping to reach a broader demographic. Of course, it was a risk given that the vineyard dated back decades, and was a staple in the area.

We didn't need the facelift, and it did worry me slightly that people would reject the new feel but, with my dad's retirement, and me stepping in to fill his very large shoes, I wanted to create my own stamp on Giordano Cellars.

I shuffled the papers on my desk, looking for my phone. Still groggy, I flipped on the camera and shook my head. Mascara settled under my eyes giving me a nineties goth look that was severely at odds with my once-crisp white button-down shirt and floral scarf.

I straightened up, stretching my arms over my head. The simple movement helped release some of the tension in my body. Taking a long walk through the vines later would relax the rest of me.

The door creaked open below. I smiled when I heard the tell-tale sounds of my dog, Olive, rolling across the sandy floor, the little bell dinging on the cart she used to help her walk. When I adopted her, the vet suggested amputating her bum leg, but when it was casted, she didn't take to three-legged walking like many animals do. The little wheelie-cart that carried her non-working hind part was the perfect, though often squeaky, solution.

"Morning," I said, turning to the noise behind me.

"You've got to stop sleeping out here," Mac chided, as she

climbed up the spiral wrought-iron staircase. Moments later she reached the second floor of the old barn that served as our offices. She gave me a once-over and shook her head disapprovingly at my dark brown hair that was in a state of waywardness. "That's an interesting look. My Chemical Romance meets Banana Republic."

I made a hand gesture that my Nonna would be upset about. "Hand it over, I need it." "A thank you would be nice."

"I owe you, that's always better than a thank you."

"You've got an office in the main building next door, in case you forgot. It even has heat, you know, since it's the winter in the Northeast. Oh, and an ergonomic chair. A cappuccino machine that would supply this little delight for you whenever you needed it," she teased in the sweetest voice, kicking the milk crate I used for a seat. She held out a slightly dented thermos.

"Thanks," I said, taking a much-needed sip. "But you know that I don't work as well in that office. I like the bite of the fresh air. Besides when Giordano's was started, this was the office. I feel a connection to the barn that I don't have anywhere else. It feels like the old Italian vineyards where the family is from."

"I get that but if you used the good office, I wouldn't have to come outside in the freezing cold and climb a ladder to talk to you."

I eyed her blonde hair, up in a fancy twist that was at odds with her casual skinny jeans and a camel coat. "Eh, you have the time... Besides fresh air is good for you and it's not that bad out."

"It's thirty degrees, Ello."

"Okay but I have the space heater, and the blanket you crocheted for me last Christmas, and Olive likes sleeping in the sun that comes in through the window."

"All solid points, but you're avoiding the most important part..." "Whatever do you mean."

"You had a date last night, yet, there's no sign of him this morning." She looked around in her own theatric way as if some guy was going to jump out as if he'd been caught.

I attempted to look innocent, widening my eyes and looking away shyly but gave up the pretense when she laughed. "Yes, I did have company and he was nice, but so boring. Like, plain toast boring. I know you think I need to get out there—"

She interrupted with her hand shooting up. "You *do* need to get out there. I think you pick unappealing men to date so that you can use it as an excuse to not get into a relationship."

"I do not!" I said a little too loudly.

Mac ignored my outburst. "You know I've been trying to set you up with the perfect—"

I clapped my hands together. "Oh, I almost forgot, did you see that list of potential food truck options for that spring event?"

"Yes, why? And stop trying to change the subject."

"What do you think? Will they bring in the under-forty crowd?"

She looked at me skeptically. "What's wrong with the over-forty crowd? They're our bread and butter."

I balked. "Nothing! I don't mean it as a slight. I love them, and their eagerness to come to tastings and events. I'm just trying to find a way to entice people our age to come out, too. Mix and mingle and become lifetime customers too. We can't seem to compete against the beer joints and if we want to grow..."

"I agree with that. It was something your father never really had a handle on. The twenties and thirties demographic always escaped us ."

"So, The Pasta Queen and The Crooked Lobster food trucks will do the trick?" I said, smiling. "They're always at the brewing company with long lines."

"Yes that sounds good—Now..." Mac narrowed her eyes and pointed her finger at me. "Let's circle back to the original subject that you conveniently decided to change.."

"I have no idea what you're talking about," I said innocently, stacking the papers on the corner of my desk. I tipped the small canning jar that I used for a vase toward the window hoping the winter sun might help the blooms stay alive. I looked up to take in the view from the barn window. It highlighted what was the best view of the entire vineyard, at least in my opinion. Rows upon rows of grapes, outbuildings dotted throughout the expanse of the property.

I smiled and took a big sip of coffee. "What's on the agenda for today besides the meeting that I'm going to be late for?"

"I'll push the meeting back fifteen minutes because you need a shower to fix—that," she said, pointing aggressively to my hair. "Then we're meeting to discuss the Valentine's Day event."

I mock-gagged.

Mac pointed her finger at me. "You promised that after how successful the Christmas event was that we would do it again. The next logical holiday is Valentine's Day."

"I know what I said, but Christmas was different. It's festive and cozy and magical.

Valentine's Day is just so cliche."

"Of course *you* would say that, but put your sad, empty love life aside for a minute." "Hey!"

"This is a business Ello, and love and wine are synonymous. Don't you love the idea of two people finding love on Valentine's Day at your family's vineyard? It's the best advertising money can buy."

"What if we save the advertising money for St. Patrick's Day instead?"

Her mouth flattened into a thin, disapproving line. "Yes, because nothing says, 'Celebrate the Irish' like Italian wine."

"Easter?" I offered.

"What? Tell me you're joking."

I shrugged. "It's a new direction. It's not sacramental wine but I mean, we can do it up all fancy for Jesus."

Mac looked exasperated, her eyes wide and her head tipped to the side.

At this point, I was just messing with her. I knew full well my ideas sounded ridiculous. Intellectually I knew this event was going to be great for business. Valentine's Day was one of the most profitable celebrations at the vineyard. The wine sales alone could carry us for a quarter. Not to mention the many engagements that happened here, which led to a slew of social media posts that we got tagged in throughout the entire month of February. From a business standpoint, I loved February and Valentine's Day. But from my own perspective, I was a Valentine's Day Grinch.

"I know we need to do the event, Mac. But I do want to

put it on the record that the thought of single people gathering on Valentine's Day makes me cringe for them. I used to be one of those people, but not anymore."

My best friend, and the company's head of marketing wasn't paid nearly enough to deal with me. Especially the under-caffeinated me. She sighed dramatically. "Think of it this way.

Didn't you *just* tell me that you're trying to get in *our* age demo? This is *literally* what our age group wants to do. Get tipsy and get plowed."

"Is that the name of the event?"

She groaned in frustration. "I can't with you."

"'Get Plowed At The Vinyard' Everyone likes a good pun! How about putting it on t- shirts? Or our coasters for the tasting rooms?"

"Focus, Ello!"

She pulled a folder from under her arm. Opening it, she showed me the first page. "They won't love it as much as they'll love an intimate evening celebration called '*Love at the Vineyard.*'"

"Get Plowed sounds better."

Mac threw her hands in the air. "I'm going to toss you off this barn one day. It tracked well with the mailing list, the online social surveys and our friends. And they're the ones coming

and paying a pretty penny for it next month, so you'll just sit there, looking fabulous and welcoming *our age group* in with a smile."

"Begrudgingly," I added.

"Listen, Ello, you have to look at the bigger picture." I

rolled my eyes as she started in on me with her "look at the bigger picture" motto. One would think she should be a motivational speaker and not a marketing maven. Despite my eye roll, she continued on as if she didn't even see it. "You can wear a LOVE STINKS shirt under your coat for all I care, just look the part. We're getting a metric ton of press out of this shindig."

Mac began climbing down the ladder.

"Cupid rhymes with stupid you know," I blurted, and she paused, popping her head back up over the ledge.

"Pardon?"

I glared. "Don't pretend like you didn't hear me."

"Oh, I'm not pretending," she smiled. "I heard you loud and clear. I just want to know what you're thinking."

"I'm thinking that I know I have to be there but I don't have to like it." "Do you really not like the event?" she said sounding hurt.

Crap. Not only was I a bad boss, but I was also being a bad friend. "No, that's not it. Forget everything I said. I was having fun teasing you and I took it too far—and I'm sorry for that. The event you've planned is going to be amazing. I'm looking forward to seeing all our friends and having a fun night out."

"And almost all of them are coming to this event. Not just because I'm making them, but because they really want to."

"Well not really..." I side eyed her to make sure I wasn't venturing into bad-friend territory again. Her eyes were narrowed, and her lip was pulled between her teeth. A sign that Mac was deep in thought. It was better than her being mad at me so I kept going. "Technically, Ashley is only coming because of the free wine and Josh is coming because he's off of work for the first weekend in three months and we haven't seen him in ages."

"Go on," she said.

"Well, Xavier doesn't have time for a relationship. He and Lucy are so busy with work. They tell us all the time they don't need a significant other. I don't know if the event is going to be up their alley but they're supportive, and I think they want to get tipsy."

"Yeah, yeah, right. I think you might be onto something. Even I have to admit that not everyone loves Valentine's Day. Some people are like you and are anti-love."

"I have an idea!" I yelled at her. Her and Olive froze since they weren't used to me being so animated in the morning. "Let me throw some stuff down on paper and I'll meet you in the conference room."

"Ah has the love bug bit you?" Mac asked as she continued climbing down the ladder. "Please, I'm a natural repellant."

When she reached the bottom, she shouted up. "One day, your cynical ass will be handed to you by someone tall, dark and handsome and I hope to God, I'm there to see it."

2

Chapter Two

In an hour, I had thrown together a separate event from Love at the Vineyard—the event that Mac had spent months organizing. When the rest of us were elbow deep in wrapping paper during Christmas, she was designing a tasting menu of our signature reds that paired with chocolates from a local shop in town. Her head was fully immersed in all things Valentine's Day and normally, I was relieved to have her deal with it. But now with my new idea, I was entering her territory. Did I really think I could pull this off? Sure Mac had spent weeks putting this together, but I knew enough to put together a quick and dirty event, didn't I?

Mentally filing away "Quick and Dirty" as a potential future party theme, I settled back into the conference room with a large cup of coffee, and a bagel smeared with home-made jam. It had been made by friends from a neighboring farm, and we sold them in our store along with other local wares.

While I stirred a heaping amount of sugar into my coffee

mug, my eyes wandered around the space. "I must say, this is a nice room."

"This is precisely why you should spend more time over here. Enjoy the nice, warm rooms."

I gave Mac a small smile. It felt odd to be in a place I had virtually grown up in and not feel comfortable there. "I know, I know."

She nodded and petted Olive who was napping on her bed in the corner, then moved on to straighten one of the photos on the wall that didn't really need to be adjusted. Tinkering and fussing were also things Mac did when she was thinking.

"So, you mentioned an idea..." She took a seat across from me and smiled expectantly. "I got to thinking when you mentioned that not everyone loves Valentine's Day, and

that people are in different places in their lives. You and I are looking for something completely different. So is everyone else in the world, so why limit ourselves to *one* Valentine's Day event?"

"Okay..." she said curiously. "What are you getting at exactly? Having the event go all weekend?"

I shook my head. "No, it would still happen on one night but we will have two events." "Two."

"Yep, two. Before your head spins around, let me explain. Love at the Vineyard is planned within an inch of its life. We're going to focus now on an Anti-Valentine's Day event."

"Anti?"

"Well, not exactly. It'll be an alternative celebration and maybe something to bring in the under forty crowd, which you know I've been trying to do. People that aren't looking for their one true love can hang out and just be social with like-minded people. If something happens, well that's a bonus but the main focus is embracing singledom. Friends are just as important as anything else on Valentine's Day so let's celebrate that too."

She smiled. "Leslie Knope would be proud. It's like Galentine's Day but for everyone." "Yeah, I mean why not. What did my dad always say, 'plan for everything.' That's what

this could be. Everyone is included."

"Genius, Ello. Genius! What do we need to do to get started?" I handed her a hastily made mockup of the new event.

"It's not as planned out and intricate as your event, but I don't think that will be an issue. We already have food and wine, what more can you need?"

She laughed. "While I think this is a fantastic idea, I worry that there is not enough time to pull this altogether. I still have the Love in the Vineyard event to work on and all that marketing..."

"Hey! Relax, it's fine. I've got it. I'll handle it. You continue on planning the Love in the Vineyard event and I'll handle the Anti-Love event."

She rolled her eyes. "You're going to call it the Anti-Love event?"

I shrugged. "I'm sure I can come up with something better. There's plenty of time." "Okay... but just keep in mind that if you want to do this other bash, you have to run it. I

can't with everything else, especially when the Love at the Vineyard event is happening simultaneously."

"I already figured that and I'm ready to roll up my sleeves."

She frowned. "I don't want to rain all over your Anti-Love

parade, but event planning really isn't your forte. Remember what happened last time? I still get social media comments about the black roses at the bridal shower."

I shrugged. "It was an honest mistake. Blush and black are basically the same word and you write like a chicken."

"Oh, sure. I'm guessing it had *nothing to do with* the fact that the shower in question was for Michelle McConnell, your high school nemesis."

I waved her away. "It was an honest mistake. And having black roses at a shower is not *that* bad. It wasn't like it was her wedding. And anyway, Michelle McConnell can suck it after all the things she used to do to me back in high school."

"She really was horrible to you. But seriously though, I can't be in two places at once and need you there. Having these two events could potentially double our profit for February. Can you swing it? I can call someone to assist."

I normally didn't handle the events. My job mainly entailed dealing with distributors and all things associated with selling and growing wine. And I wasn't the best people person so the idea of the event hanging on my shoulders made me cringe.

"You know, I can get my friend to help. I can call in the one that I keep trying to set you up with?" she offered when I didn't answer her, and I knew where she was headed. This guy again, Madonna mia! His sister was an old friend of hers and Mac has been going on about him ever since he apparently became single.

"No I don't need any help. I'll be there for the event. Oh, look, Dating Disaster Bingo!" "Keep changing the subject, Ello."

"It's a gift."

"Smart ass," she said, stacking the papers up and dropping them into a folder. "Let's get started on this. We only have a month to pull two stellar events together."

3

Chapter Three

"Mac, you're making me nervous. Call me back!" I shouted into the phone.

"She's never late. And certainly, never on a day when two events are taking place," I shouted at the caterer. The poor woman backed away, eyes wide and hands up. It was just that we had a month to plan these events and everything was going as planned. Until today.

"I'm sorry, I'm just panicked. Has anyone heard from Mac?" My voice was shrill, palms sweating and throat dry. There were a few people left in the office, all of whom shook their heads.

Someone gasped, and I turned. Leaning against the door frame was Mac. Ashen with her hair in total disarray, her clothes were rumpled and covered in *something*. "What the hell happened?"

Her hand flew to her mouth a second too late. At least she aimed for the garbage can. The sounds were wretched.

Someone made a choked sound and a few people barreled out of the office and into the hallway.

I ran to her, unsure of what to do except to hold her long, wild hair back from her face. "I'm sorry," she said, wiping her hand across her mouth then down her sweats. "I've

been sick for hours. I think it's food poisoning," she mumbled just before getting sick again.

One hand was holding her hair, and the other should have been patting her on the back in a comforting fashion, but instead, it was holding my nose, so I too didn't get sick.

When there was a slight reprieve, I helped her up and ushered her into the small office kitchen. After setting her down into a chair, I fetched a couple paper towels and a glass of water. "Here, small sips."

She shook her head at the glass, her coloring now a light green. She took the paper towel and wiped her forehead. "I can't. The second something hits my stomach, it launches back up like a rocket."

"What the hell did you eat?" I asked.

Her lips were a thin line, before they curled in as if she was going to be sick again. I grabbed the closest garbage can and set it in front of her. "Just in case. So, what do you think caused you to get sick?"

The green hue of her skin was darkening and I wondered if it meant she was going to be sick again. *It was.*

When she stopped, she leaned back and breathed in through her nose and out her mouth. "I had leftovers," she said weakly. "Seafood alfredo,"

"Seafood alfredo? No, not the same one from last week?"

"I was tired and hungry and I didn't want to wait thirty minutes for Door Dash to deliver."

"You should have waited!"

"Don't judge me when I'm sick. I've been working so hard and I didn't have time to grocery shop." Her voice cracked and her eyes welled up with tears.

I wrapped my arm around her. "I know you work hard—now your only job is to take care of you. Don't worry about anything. I'll handle the party."

"I'm sorry, Ello. I'm sure I'll feel better soon. But now I just want to sleep," she said and laid her head on the small kitchen table. To punctuate her point, she was lightly snoring a second later.

"Come on, killer. We have to get you out of here," I said, hauling her up and wrapping my arm around her waist for support.

We paused at the door. Her teary, bloodshot eyes were fixed on the wall where the announcement that ran in the local paper for our dueling events was hanging. "I'm so sorry. What are you going to do about tonight?"

I plastered on a smile. "I'll make it work like I always do."

Meanwhile, I was running through all of the worst-case scenarios that were likely going to happen because there was no way I could be in two places at once.

***

When the Giordanos first came to America and bought this land in the Hudson Valley for the vineyard, they also built a small house to live in, so they were never too far from the business. At some point, every generation had lived in the same small two-story house on the outskirts of the property. It bordered the untouched wooded area that we also owned but

hadn't developed as of yet. It was peaceful, and mine, and for tonight at least, it would be home to a very sick, and totally out of it, Mac.

An hour after practically carrying Mac into my house to rest up, I was showered and trying to work magic on my hair and makeup. "Thank God, I live on the property or I would be totally screwed," I said to Olive who had just wiggled her adorable self into my bedroom.

"My little Olive, do you want to come to the party with Momma?" I said in a sing-song voice. She wagged her tail in response to everything, so I took that as a yes. "Come on, we'll check on Auntie Mac later."

When I descended the stairs into my front yard, Olive used the small ramp I installed so she could get in and out of the house easily. I looked to both sides of the vineyard. Lights from the events were visible in the darkening sky.

The events were on opposite sides of the property. Which, under original circumstances would have been fine because we were each going to oversee one, but now, with Mac down for the count, I was on double-duty. Thank God for the golf cart.

Nestled in the corner of my car port, and beneath a large tarp, sat an ancient golf cart. It was somewhere in the vicinity of fifteen years old which in golf cart terms meant it was one hundred. There were strips of peeling duct tape on the doors, a couple questionable stickers on the back bumper that my dad left and a specialized seatbelt harness, that I, of course, had lovingly installed for my dog.

I placed Olive gently into passenger seat and buckled her in so she wouldn't slide out.

Once secure, we took off toward the Anti-Valentine's Day event in my old barn. Did I go overboard? Not in decorations, which looked fantastic. I called in my black rose vendor again— having finally found an appropriate venue for their wares—and mixed them with bloody arrow centerpieces. The games, however, may have been overly planned. But I really wanted to make sure the added event was just as successful as the original, and I felt like too many activities was was still better than too few.

When I arrived at the old barn, the DJ was already set up on the first floor and had the music roaring through the massive propped open doors. It was reminiscent of the scene in *The Wedding Singer* when Adam Sandler let loose at the wedding reception singing LOVE STINKS. I

straightened my red cardigan sweater that was over my sparkly *YOU WISH* t-shirt and adjusted my broken heart belt. What can I say, overboard was my middle name.

The caterers were bringing a wide selection of hor d'oeuvres that would be passed around by servers who were wearing the Anti-Valentine's Day T-shirts I'd had printed with a silhouette of Cupid lying dead, shot by his own arrows. Had I gone too heavy on the murdery vibes? Oh well, too late now.

The catering van was parked a bit cock-eyed against the extra tent we set up, the front end sticking out in a way that made it impossible to see if anyone was behind the van as I pulled up.

Unfortunately, as I zipped into a free spot where I could park the golf cart alongside the barn to make it easy to run between events without getting blocked in, I bumped into someone. *Literally.*

"Whoa, there," he said, backing up and rubbing his thigh where the bumper, barely, tapped him. "Golf carts may look innocent but they're dangerous."

My first instinct was to ask why he was here already, since the event didn't start for another half hour, but that would be rude, and I did just hit him with a golf cart.

"Are you hurt?" I said, and smiled apologetically. I slipped out of the seat and gently unstrapped Olive and picked her up. No one could resist her. Placing her on the ground, she scooted over to him wagging her tail.

"No, I'm not hurt. Maybe my pride a little for not being agile enough to dodge a rickety old golf cart."

"I'll have you know this is a precious family heirloom."

He eyed my dad's old bumperstickers and suddenly the one that said "Weekend Hooker" beneath a fishing pole seemed way more embarrassing than it had moments earlier.

I watched as he kneeled beside Olive to scratch her head, which only made her tail wag faster. When she got that excited, the wheeled cart shook and made a squeaky sound letting everyone know how happy she was. Laughing, he braced his hands on his knees and pushed off to stand at his full height.

"So anyway, hello there," I said awkwardly, and rolled back on my heels.

If someone asked me if I thought this man was attractive, I would have tripped over the words trying to explain just how good-looking he was. Thick dark hair that was just a smidge too long because it curled at the edges of his ears. Dark eyes that were framed with equally dark lashes and two very adorable dimples that were on full display because he was smiling at me while I was blatantly ogling him. He wasn't traditionally handsome. It wasn't boyish good looks, but a ruggedness. Even in the dead of winter, his skin held a slight tan that highlighted the tiny lines near his eyes.

But, for as physically attractive as he was, there was an underlying confidence that rolled off of him. He stood with his shoulders back, and casually leaned against the golf cart like he was the heartthrob in a teen movie. It didn't work for every guy but this one was actually pulling it off, and I was loving the eyecandy. Until he cleared his throat and rubbed the scruff on his jaw, and I was reminded of the fact that I was ogling him quite obviously.

"Sorry," I said, rocking back on my heels again. "About? The bump, or the staring?"

My cheeks burned, and I curled my lips in trying not to smile. "Sorry about the cart bump and I guess for the staring as well."

"No big deal on the bump," he said easily, brushing a hand through his dark hair. "The staring is an interesting development."

"Yes, well I am nothing if not interesting."

"It certainly seems so." He gave me a half smile that made my stomach do a flip. "Not to be rude but if you're here for the party, you're about a half hour too early."

He stood. "I am?" He glanced at his watch. "Crap. I guess I am. I thought it would have taken me longer to get here."

Looking behind him, I spied the servers getting out of their cars and tying their aprons on, the Valentine's Day wait staff clad in red and the Anti-Valentines crew in black. I frowned. I needed to get moving or I would be late. "Come on, Olive."

"Where are you going?"

"I have to be at two places at once and have to stop here before heading somewhere else. Not enough hours in the night, I'm afraid," I apologized.

The caterers were starting to hurry between the barn and the main event space. It made it difficult to chat privately any longer.

In my pocket I always carried a business card with a free bottle of wine offer on the back. It also had my name and number on the front. Just in case.

I slipped the card into his hand. "No hard feelings?"

He glanced at the back of the card. "Wow, you're plying me with free wine, and that's it?" he said, pocketing it without flipping it over to see my name, Eloisa Giordano, President.

"What else would I offer?" I asked, realizing too late that my voice sounded flirty.

Abort, abort!

He narrowed his eyes and grinned, leaning casually against the golf cart again. Damn that did work for him.

"I'm not sure. What else is on the table?" he said, and I felt like I was going to go up in

flames.

I made an awkward choked sound. "Oh, shit. My flirting game is abysmal it seems. Out of practice. I just meant, I didn't want any hard feelings hence the free wine, but then it came out sounding sexual—not that there's anything wrong with being sexual but we've only just met so it seems way too soon for that and wow...I am bad at this."

He looked down at his shoes, and when his eyes met mine again, he smiled. "I don't know, I don't think you're bad at it. Perhaps, I can find you when you're not so busy and we can chat? I mean, this is the event for getting to know people, right?"

"No, it's not actually."

He frowned. "It's not? I thought Giordano's was hosting a Valentine's event tonight?" "We are. Two actually. This isn't the love fest. This is the well, it's the non-love fest." "I'm afraid I'm confused."

"Forgive me, I made you that way. You see, this barn has the Anti-Valentine's Day soiree. For anyone that is perfectly happy being single, and isn't quite ready to mingle. The other event is in the event space in the main building. That way," I said, pointing to the direction of the other building. "Although, this one will be more fun."

He laughed. "If you say so."

My hands flew to my hips. A move he noticed and countered with his arms crossing over his broad chest. "I'll have you know, it will be great, so help me I'll make sure of it."

"You're determined, I applaud you for that. I'm sure it'll be a fun evening for all involved," he said, holding up a pink ticket for the Love at the Vineyard event. "Just not the one I signed up for."

"You mean, you don't want to stay and listen to anti-love anthems all night?" "Hmm, tempting but I'm afraid I'm in the wrong place."

"And don't forget early."

"I'm always early. It's one of my superpowers..."

I nodded. "I like that strategy. I may adopt it for myself."

"You're welcome to it. That being said, I must be off to the correct shindig so I am not late. You never know who you'll meet when you show up before the crowd." He gave a sweet little parting shrug and started to turn around.

I shouldn't have wanted him to stay, but, something about him was interesting to me. Okay, it was his hotness. His hotness was *very* interesting to me. "You're more than welcome to stay here, even though your ticket is for the other one. I know the owner, I think you'll be okay."

He looked over his shoulder and I gave him a wink. A wink. Me! Who was I and where had I been hiding?

He laughed and placed the empty glass, and fork onto a passing tray. "It is tempting but alas, Love in the Vineyard is calling my name. Must be the hopeless romantic in me. Any idea where it is?"

"Yes, let me point you in the right direction." I took a deep breath. What was I doing? I didn't believe in finding love on Valentine's Day. I shook my head to clear my own silliness.

"It's really not too far and I want to make sure you get your money's worth. Good thing you bumped into me, huh?"."

He laughed. "I believe *you* bumped into *me.*"

"Tomato, tom*ah*to. Follow me."

I walked to the end of the Anti-Valentine's Day tent and pointed toward the opposite end of the rows and rows of leafless winter vines. "You're going to follow the path labeled Chardonnay. There are plenty of lights woven through the stakes, so you don't have to worry about getting lost. At the other end, you'll find your love. I mean, *your* Love at the Vineyard event that you signed up for." I laughed awkwardly.

If he caught my discomfort, he ignored it choosing instead to turn back to me. His eyes moved over my face, and I felt the heat rise to my cheeks again. Damn heaters.

"I hope you enjoy your evening and find what you're looking for," I said. "I hope we both do."

I held out my hand. Formal goodbye, after all it was nice to meet him. He took my hand gently between his, and lifted it up to his lips. His eyes held mine as he dropped the faintest kiss onto my skin.

"What—" my question was cut off when one of the servers dropped a tray, sending it clattering to the ground.

"Oh, I should help," I apologized, and pointed again to the route he needed to take. "The path, don't forget to stay on Chardonnay."

I turned, taking a few steps away with Olive following me with her cart. The urge to look back was strong. Using my hair as a shield, I tipped my head back and saw him standing there, smiling.

When he saw me turn, he waved before backing away slowly, his eyes not leaving mine. I waited until I couldn't see his smile anymore.

Damn flutters.

4

Chapter Four

An hour later and the event had started. Inside the barn, I checked in with the caterer, some of the wait staff, the DJ and the bartender. Folks were starting to arrive, mostly dressed casually—except for one woman who was in a black, vintage ball gown with a massive hoop skirt, and uncomfortable-looking heels. She carried a black lacy parasol and wore dainty gloves on both hands.

"That's really something," one of my employees, Lynn, said, coming up to stand beside me. A couple people milled about, looking surprisingly cheery considering this was the Anti- Valentine's Day party. The music was loud, the food looked delicious, but the majority of the people were not talking, with the exception of my friends that came. Though, they were only conversing with each other. The game stations I'd set up around the room sat vacant, and there was zero mingling. It made for a bit of an awkward scene.

I coaxed Josh and Ashley over to the bar and got them started on a game of Head's Up against Xavier and

Lucy. Then I encouraged another group of five to play a game of Cards Against Humanity, hoping even more would follow suit.

I angled my head to the woman in black. "I give her credit coming to an event dressed like that. If she's comfortable in it, good for her."

Trish, another long time employee who was working the event came over to us. She looked worried. "Eloisa, hardly anyone is at any of the game tables. They're either at the bar, headed to the bar, or just left the bar."

"The dirty Scrabble may have also not been great. Head's Up seems to be the only one with any interested parties, but they also look like they're ready to fight," Lynn said.

"They're my friends, they'll be fine. They haven't fought since Thanksgiving." "Somehow that isn't exactly reassuring. What are we going to do?"

"Is it too dorky?" I asked, seeing a couple of women bypass the jumbo connect four board that was on the floor. I really thought people would love this event, but now in hindsight I realized that this event needed more than games to be a fun event. But what? Wasn't Anti- Love reason enough to have a party?

Another shrug from both Trish and Lynn. "The other event has games, right?" "Sort of. It's more getting to know you type of stuff. Like speed dating without the urgency and it's fueled by wine."

"Too bad we weren't stationed over there," Trish muttered.

Great. Even my staff would rather be at the other event. "You might be soon if this keeps being depressing." Sure, it wasn't supposed to be a hook-up event, but I thought, hoped, people would at least socialize.

Something needed to happen. "Have the DJ start asking some questions. Maybe it'll loosen things up a bit."

"Like what?"

"Bad Date Bingo? Never Have I Ever? Do whatever you need to do—just get people talking. And for the love of all things holy, get them drinking!"

Trish shrugged. "That I can do."

"Hey, I have to head over to the other event. I have my cell on me so if you need anything call and I'll fly right back over," I explained to them both. "I should be back in say thirty minutes or so."

"It's not like there's a ton going on here, no worries. We've got it handled," Lynn said, and I tried not to frown.

Maybe I had gone too overboard with the anti-love sentiments, but it was supposed to be about being single and being good with that choice. Hanging out with friends and not having the pressure of love, love, love. Why had it turned out to be so depressing?

I made my exit while Lynn tried—unsuccessfully—to keep a couple of women from leaving by plying them with wine. "Thanks anyway, Lynn, live and learn. Come on, Olive. Let's go check out the happy people."

Once Olive was safely buckled up, we took off on the dirt and pebble path toward the main house. Driving up to it always took my breath away. Mac had really outdone herself on the renovations last year. It wasn't as classic, and rustic, as the old barn on the property, but it was a different sort of sight to behold.

Two tall field stone pillars wrapped in vines welcomed you onto the land where we built the main building. A fence wrapped around it giving it its own secluded feel within the center of the massive acreage.

The house itself was a massive white structure with tall black doors and an ambiance that was both elegant and rustic.

It was nestled in the heart of our raspberry field. In the summer, the air around it smelled like fresh raspberries all season long. Though the smell had faded now, in the dead of winter, the magic of being in the middle of a vineyard that was just about to turn green again, and the twinkling fairy lights did make it the perfect spot for the Love at the Vineyard event.

Cars were lined up along the fence, indicating just how many tickets were sold. I picked up Olive, and once she was on the gravel, she scooted along behind me as we entered the stately black doors.

The place was transformed into something beautiful. Mac had a knack for the details, and she left no stone unturned for this one.

Tall round bistro-style tables were placed around the center of the large room usually used for weddings and tasting parties. The DJ was set up on the edge of the dance floor and playing Taylor Swift favorites—nothing like the anti-love anthems we had playing at the old barn. There were two bars set up where you could sample the wine before you had a full glass. Both were filled with people who were chatting amiably while waiting their turn.

Just like the other event, servers passed around culinary delights that paired perfectly with our wines. What was vastly different though, was that these party-goers were socializing, smiling, laughing and dancing.

And, there were at least three times as many people here.

There were tables set up with various getting-to-know-you games in each corner of the expansive room. Near the DJ, people were choosing random songs from a bowl. They then had to read the lyrics, not sing them, and hope that their randomly chosen partner would guess the popular song.

A few were playing a chocolate memory game where one person was blindfolded and then had to sample chocolate, decide what brand it was, and then put them into alphabetical

order. Sounded simple enough, but after a glass or three or wine, it wasn't as easy as originally thought.

A handful of people were getting started with ring around the roses, which basically had people spinning strangers, who then tried to arrange roses in a vase. Again, harder than it seemed when wine was involved.

Overall, the balloons seemed bigger, the floral centerpieces looked bolder and brighter and of course, the Valentine's staple, candy hearts were hopeful and loving, not moody and discouraging...or murdery. Basically, the opposite of the ones

I had for the Anti-Valentine event that said things like *Swipe Left*, *I'll Pass*, and *You Suck*, these were classics—*I Like You*, *You're Cute*, *Let's Dance*.

The mood was hopeful, and if I were being honest with myself, contagious.

A master of ceremonies was tapping the microphone to get started on some of the festivities but there appeared to be a sound issue. He disappeared off behind some draperies with the DJ.

I pulled out my phone and snapped a few photos that we would use for the website and other press materials. I also sent a quick text to check on Mac but also to tell her job well done. Pushing the microphone, I dictated the text. "I have to hand it to you, this is exceptional.

P.S. I hope you're not dead."

Someone sidled up beside me as I ended the dictation and pushed send. "I hope they're not dead either." The guy from earlier was standing beside me, arms crossed over his chest, and he was smiling.

"Eavesdropping isn't very nice."

"Neither is hitting someone with a golf cart. Consider us even now. What's up with your not-dead friend?" he asked before dropping to his knees and giving Olive some back scratches – much to her delight.

"My best friend. She's down for the count with some food poisoning so I was just checking on her."

"Ah, that's kind of you," he said, standing up and assuming the same position. "She's supposed to be here too."

"Stinks that she's missing it. The food is very good, and the wine isn't so bad either. I look forward to getting my free bottle later."

I fought back a grin. "I suggest the Gewurz- traminer."

"God bless you. Wait, was that not a sneeze?"

I snick- ered. "You're not a wine enthusiast I take it?" He shrugged. "I like a glass with dinner."

"A smooth pinot noir with a nice steak?" I said, getting hungry just thinking of it. "Yes, exactly. Or a Bordeaux with some rich and hearty pasta."

"Hmm, now we're talking."

"So," we both said at the same time, and then I smiled awkwardly.

"Want to try a game?" I offered, surprising myself. I hadn't planned on partaking, but why not have a bit of fun.

He seemed surprised at my offer, but smiled. "Sure, I love a good competition."

My eyebrow raised in challenge. "I should warn you, I'm wildly competitive. You might want to surrender in advance."

"Challenge accepted, I think I can handle you."

The nervous or excited heart flutters didn't come, this was something different. A full wave of heat barreled up my spine and right to my cheeks.

"Deal," I replied. "I'll even let you choose the game."

On each table was a pink rectangular-shaped paper that listed the activities. His dark eyes moved over it quickly. I knew he found a winner when his eyes grew wide and a devlish smile twisted up his lips.

"You're not serious," I said when he pointed to his choice. "Not the kiss and tell game, or the get drunk and screw bingo?"

"I'm sensing you were interested in a more *animated* game?"

I laughed. "What? No, I just figured –"

He shrugged. "You said it was my choice. I chose the one that I thought I would dominate at."

"So you're saying you're not a good kisser?"

He threw his head back and laughed, deep and raspy. "That's quite the challenge, I admit I'm intrigued by your line of questioning. Maybe I should rethink my choice. Make it something that highlights my other talents."

I narrowed my eyes. "Candy heart alphabetizing is flexing your mental muscles. I'm not one to back down. Let's go."

I waved one of the game hostesses over to get us set up. He stood across the bistro table from me, his eyes fixed on the glass jar of candy hearts in front of him.

He rubbed his chin.

"You look nervous," I challenged. "Nah, this will be a cake walk."

The game sounded easier than it was. Holly, the hostess, was timing us and truth be told, I struggled with remembering the alphabet, which was sad and disappointing as I hadn't had any wine.

"This is absurdly difficult. I'm an avid golfer for pity's sake. My hand-eye coordination is better than this."

I laughed. "It's more about quick thinking and speed. Golf doesn't strike me as particularily fast-paced. That might be why you're tanking."

"I'll have you know that golf is wildly competive and, son of a bitch, I am tanking."

By the time the buzzer went off, we each had at least five or six hearts left and neither of us had done a great job of alphabetizing them.

"Why did we think anyone could do this drunk, if you guys can't do it sober?" Holly said as she scooped the candies back into the individual glass jars.

"I call it a tie," I offered, holding my hand out. "A tie it is."

We stood, side by side, taking stock in the festivities before us. From this vantage point, I could see him out of my periphery. Every few seconds he would glance over and smile.

In an effort not to grin in response, I focused on trying to make out the images on his partially exposed tattoo.

"Why are you smiling?" he asked, his voice was low. He kept his eyes fixed straight ahead versus looking over at me to wait for my answer.

"I'm trying not to."

His tongue peeked out, wetting his bottom lip. "Why are you trying not to? You've got a lovely smile."

"You know, you're making this difficult. I'm supposed to be immune to charming and flirty men."

Finally, he turned, giving me the full weight of his smile. "Ah, and who is this charming and flirty man that you're interested in?

I took a step back. "Who said I was interested?"

He matched my retreat by coming forward a hint. "Maybe I'm hoping that you are."

I forced myself not to look away. No matter how much my face burned, or how badly I wanted to smile, I was a stone-cold Valentine's Day grinch and Mr. Chardonnay wasn't going to to force me to succumb to mushiness.

"There's a lot to unpack there."

"Excuse me?" I looked at him in confusion. "You said all of that out loud," he said calmly. "Crap." I slapped a hand over my mouth.

"Let's start with the nickname, I like it. We'll keep it and give you one too, *Ms. Grinch..*

Two, what has Valentine's Day ever done to you to make you hate it so much?"

"I...Well..." I tried to think of the best way to answer him and decided on the truth. "My father loved Valentine's Day and made a big deal out of it every year for my mother and I. But then my mom left us both when I was sixteen...on Valentine's Day."

His eyes grew so wide, I wished I could say "gotcha" to show that my sob story was not true. But it was very real and a memory that I had never spoken about before today to anyone, not even Mac. Maybe it was because he was a stranger, or maybe it was because it was Valentine's Day and there was still a part of me that wanted to have hope in a possible romance on the most romantic night of the year, and that's why I found myself opening up to him.

"I'm sorry. That's awful...I—"

I held my hand up to stop him from going on. "It's fine. You don't have to be sorry. My dad and I survived. But every year on Valentine's Day we always had an Anti-Love Day." I smiled at the memories.

"Where's your dad now?"

"Florida, where he retired last year. He has a nice lady friend and I'm sure he's Valentine's Day-ing her up." I cringed at the mental image.

"Well at least he has someone, right?"

I nodded as we turned back into our other position—side by side, arms crossed and the two of us staring at the crowd.

"That must have been hard. I'm sorry, I'm sure I'd feel the same way."

I shrugged. "It's made me who I am." I said, and realized just how true it was. The lack of a loving relationship to learn from, formed how I saw love. "I'm guessing since you're Mr. Romance, your parents are happily married?"

"Mr. Romance, I like it," he said with a beaming smile. "And yes, they're still totally head over heels for each other."

I grinned. "That sounds perfect."

For about ten seconds, we just stared at one another and I couldn't help but wonder, what if...

"So," he finally began. "Do you want to grab something to eat? So far, everything has been a winner."

I smiled proudly. "I should hope so. It was a painstaking process to choose the menu and the wines to pair with them."

"What does that mean exactly?"

I held out my hand. "I'm the owner of Giordano Cellars."

"Oh, it's nice to meet you. You know, I got the impression you knew more about this place than you let on. Why the secrecy?"

"Isn't that the theme for us? Strangers in the night?

"I suppose you're right. So, what made you venture over to this party? The other one too wild and crazy?" he quipped.

I smirked. "Something like that. I've got to bounce between the two events. More people registered for this one, so I figured it was safe to leave that one for a while and check out the lovebirds."

"Oh, really? I was only kidding, I figured anti-love would be the real rager and people would be pretty animated."

"That was the intention," I sighed. Hearing the defeat in my voice and not liking it, I was quick to add, "But the night is still young and there's plenty of time for Anti-Love revelry!"

He didn't look entirely convinced, but he was kind enough not to call me out. Instead he walked us over toward the food and wine station. "What do you suggest we try first?"

I knew the options like the back of my hand. "The cinnamon strawberry shortcake and the sparkling brut. Fruity and earthy."

"Is that your favorite?"

I thought about it as he took two plates, and handed me one. "No, my favorite is the chocolate mousse and the sparkling red. It's like a lightning bolt to your taste buds. Remember, bite, then sip, then another bite then another sip."

The cake disappeared into his mouth. "You're right. It is like lightning." Systematically, we went through two other pairings. A peach cobbler bite with a dry

Riesling and a lemon bar with a chardonnay. I thought the latter choice was a nice nod to his nickname.

"Can I be honest?" "Please."

"I'm having a tough time getting a read on you." All the earlier humor in his voice was gone. He appeared sincerely interested.

"Really? I thought I've been an open book tonight."

"I just don't understand why you're here. I mean, I know it's your vineyard and I know you don't like Valentine's Day. I get it. But why are you at this celebration and not the other one? It seems more like your jam."

I frowned. "It was supposed to be, but it was just...so boring. I really thought an Anti- Love party would be supportive, empowering you know? A way for people to get over being

burned in crappy relationships or just to celebrate being okay with being single. Why does everything have to be about finding love all the time? I've got friends that don't want a relationship. This was for them."

"But it didn't turn out the way you expected."

I sighed. "No, it was a bit depressing if I'm being honest."

"And now you're here," he said with a satisfied smirk. "So maybe the other party being a wash was a happy twist of fate."

"You're fun to talk to, Chardonnay," I mused out loud. "Why did you call me that?"

I laughed. "I call you Mr. Chardonnay in my head. Since, that was the path I sent you down to get here."

"I thought it was because I'm sweet and full bodied."

"Perhaps, although I'd describe you as dry with a strong finish." "I believe that the lady should always finish first."

I visibly choked on my wine, and it was his turn to laugh. "I'll be sure to grab another glass of Chardonnay to try. I haven't been disappointed yet in any of the samples I had."

"That's good to hear," I said through a cough.

The MC appeared on stage again, after fixing what was wrong with the microphone. "On behalf of Giordano Cellars, I'd like to thank you all for coming tonight to the Love at the Vineyard event! Happy Valentine's Day to all of you and may cupid's arrow land on you tonight!"

I chuckled. "That's an odd way to say I hope you get lucky tonight." "Well, I guess it's how people are looking at this event."

"What do you mean?"

"Well, I guess some people are here for a quick hook up, right? Like a live Tinder event I suppose. A literal swipe-right."

I nodded. "You're right. People could be using the event that way," "I'm sensing another but."

I inhaled deeply, enjoying the fragrance of the flowers, the wine and something that must have been inherently him.

"Perhaps some aren't just looking for the one-night stand but something else. Something more?"

Mr. Chardonnay smiled as if he discovered one of my secrets. "You don't sound like someone who thinks Valentine's Day is cheesy. You sound like a romantic."

I tapped my cheek. "Ah, well you know my aversion to Valentine's Day, but now you assume I have also given up on love and relationships. You know what they say about making assumptions."

Another knee-buckling grin. This one showed off those dangerous dimples again. He rested his arms on the table beside us, leaning over it so that the candle in the center of the table, showed off the gold flecks in his brown eyes.

"Okay then, I'm casting all my assmptions aside. So what's your story?" he asked, taking the smallest step closer to me.

Taking a deep breath, I kept in mind that he was a stranger, and that I could tell him the truth, and it didn't matter what he thought.

"The truth is, my last relationship ended six months ago in complete and utter failure. I take responsibility, not for the breakup but for staying with him over a year when I knew..." I paused to let out a rueful chuckle, "I knew he wasn't the right guy for me. I caught him off guard, which is what I feel the worst about. He was literally blindsided."

My head was down but I could feel his eyes on me, watching, waiting for me to continue. "After that I began to wonder if I was meant to be in a relationship. With anyone. It really wasn't him, it was me. Sounds like a line, but it was the truth. There was nothing wrong with him, he was perfect on paper and he treated me really good. I just...when I was with him, I would have rather been alone or out with friends or working. Anything but faking it, you know? And then I'd feel really guilty, but I couldn't make my heart feel something that just wasn't there. It wasn't fair to either of us."

"And you don't think maybe it was just because he wasn't the one?" he asked softly. I shrugged. "I don't know if I believe in 'the one'."

"Hence the reason you planned the anti-love party? You've given up on it?"

I pondered that. "No, I haven't given up on it, I just know that I'm not going to settle for someone that I don't have those butterflies in my stomach for. It wouldn't be fair."

Mr. Chardonnay straightened up as a server came by and took two glasses off of the tray and laughed at the small card that was resting on it informing you of what type of wine was on each tray.

"What's so funny?" I asked. "It's Chardonnay."

"A sign, you could say," I responded, taking the glass and holding it up for a toast. "Cheers."

"What are we cheers'ing too?" "Cheers'ing? Is that a word?"

He shrugged. "It is now. So, what will the toast be?" I tapped my chin with my free hand. "To strangers."

He looked taken aback. "Strangers? Unexpected, I like it," he said with a nod.

Clinking glasses, our eyes held each other's over the glasses while we each sipped the lightly chilled wine.

Mr. Chardonnay licked his lips as he placed the glass onto the table. My eyes followed his tongue through the motion. His eyes flashed and narrowed, and his mouth slid into a wry smile. "Tonight has been all kinds of unexpected."

5

Chapter Five

As the MC was going table to table asking people random questions, I took the chance that Mr. Chardonnay, too, would be willing to share. After all, he was standing here at a Love at the Vineyard event instead of taking a girlfriend, or wife even, out for a romantic Valentine's Day. There had to be a story there.

"Since I shared, are you going to leave me hanging or are you going to tell me what made you choose to come to the Love at the Vineyard event?"

He smiled, looking down at the ticket that was on the table between us. "A friend suggested that I come. She was supposed to meet me here actually since I haven't seen her in forever."

I swallowed hard. "Oh," I said flatly, trying to keep the smile on my face. "Cool. Did she make it yet?"

Even in my own ears, I could hear that there was zero chill to my voice. I sounded irked, and I was. Not at him, but at myself for thinking this was anything other than two adults mildly flirting.

When my phone rang, I wanted to throw it into the grape press. The screen lit up with the words UNKNOWN CALLER and an unusual number. But, logically, I knew who it was.

"Hello?" I said, grateful to be saved from my newly minted awkward position.

As I suspected, it was Lynn at the other event. "Hey, Eloisa! Listen, can you stop back over? We've got a couple questions on what to do with all of this food that's leftover."

The MC was at the table beside me and was very loud. I backed away from the table to hear her better. "What do you mean leftover? The party started only an hour ago. It's even worse than when I left?"

A sleeping Olive gave me a weak noise when I picked her up to carry her out to the golf cart. Mr. Chardonnay was behind me with his hands up, questioning what was happening. I mouthed an 'I'm sorry' and left the tent, the phone propped between my head and shoulder.

"Hold on, I'll be right there. Give me ten minutes."

I buckled Olive in and tore off leaving the love songs in my dust.

By the time I arrived, the DJ had most of his equipment packed into his truck, and the caterers were collecting aprons, and had already begun cleaning up.

Trish and Lynn met me at the golf cart with cases of unopened wine in their arms. "Uh, guys? What's up?"

"Hi Eloisa," Trish began cheerfully. "We're going to just

bring all of this to the other barn and get it set up with that crew."

The menu was the same; same food and same wine so it didn't matter but, that didn't explain the need for it to be moved. "Did everyone really leave this early? I feel like we should offer refunds if everyone was so disappointed."

"Yeeeeeeah, that's not going to be necessary." She laughed. I frowned. "What do you mean?"

She leaned in. "Funny story, when you left earlier, a couple of them started pairing off." "Excuse me? Pairing off, pairing off?" I said with an arched eyebrow.

Trish nodded. "Yes, that kind of pairing off. First they were chatting and then well, the more wine they had, the looser they got. One thing led to another and they all started leaving together. Two people that didn't get together with someone here, mentioned heading over to the main house to try their luck there since they were feeling the love magic."

"I can't believe it."

"Girl, go with it. I feel like this event had the opposite effect it was supposed to. They found love after all and that's going to make for a kick ass marketing scheme once Mac finds out this event made a bunch of love connections."

"Or, at least for tonight it did," Lynn quipped as they loaded mini quiches into the van. "Well, I'll be damned. It turned into a Get Plowed party after all."

"Oh, and Mac stumbled over. We gave her some dry bread and sent her back up to your place. Hope that's okay, she looked a little worse for the wear."

I laughed. "Yeah, that's great. I'll check on her when I drop

Olive off. I'm so sorry this was an early night for you guys. I'll still pay you for the full night."

"Are you kidding?" Lynn said laughing. "We're turing our Anti-Love shirts inside out and heading over to the other event with all of this food and wine. It sounds like a blast over there."

I would've liked to say that I was surprised, but in hindsight, now that I thought about it, it made sense that the Anti-Valentines Day party had turned into a hook-up event. It wasn't the party that I'd intended, but it was the party that horny singles needed. "My job is done here," I said proudly.

I wanted to pretend I was just doing my duty and checking in on the Love at the Vineyard event, but I was actually enjoying myself over there talking to Mr. Chardonnay. I sent a text to Xavier and Lucy seeing where they were. Turned out they went to check on Mac then said they would meet me over at the main house.

It was just past eight, which meant that I had enough time to drop Olive at my house, check for myself that Mac was still breathing, and make it back to the party to make sure that everything was okay.

It totally had nothing to do with checking on Mr. Chardonnay.

"I can't believe this, Olive," I said, carrying her down the lighted pathway to my house. My home was in the same fenced in area as the old barn, which was another reason I chose to work in there versus trekking all the way down to the new offices across the vineyard.

I unlocked the front door and before I set Olive down and kissed the top of her head.

Just then, Mac appeared. "Wow," I said, as kindly as possible.

Judging by the fact that she flipped me off, I supposed it wasn't very kind. "How's it going?"

"You need new towels and floor mats in your bathroom. Maybe some paint too and definitely a hazmat suit. I'll take care of it when I don't feel like death."

My eyes grew wide, but I quickly schooled my features. "Towels? Oh, Mac, I don't care about any of that. How are you feeling? By the way, my party started out terrible but ended up okay, and I met a guy at yours."

Her head popped up. "Way to bury the lead, Giordano. Jesus Christ, what the hell did you do at my event? Who is this guy and why are you here with me and not with him? And why did your party start out terrible?" Her voice was surprisingly strong for how pale, and gaunt she looked.

"You should rest. I shouldn't have blurted all of that out," I said, backing away toward the door.

"Oh no you don't. You don't drop bombs like that and scurry off into the night. Details, and make it quick because I may have to throw up again."

I cringed. "We can wait to have a conversation about the embarrassment tomorrow." "Spill it, before I do."

Knowing that she wouldn't give it up unless I told her, I gave her the twenty-five-cent version.

"Let's see, my event sucked at first. It started off like a bad middle school dance and no one was mingling, but surprise—after a drink or two, they all ran off into the night together—presumably to bone. The end." I sketched an exaggerated bow.

"But, it's not it. You met a guy. Where?"

I took a deep breath. "He was at the wrong event and I explained how to get to the other one. We were chatting and I thought, you know what, maybe. Maybe we have something in common because he was wildly attractive and wasn't wearing a ring. And then he mentioned how his lady friend told him to come and he was waiting for her, but she didn't show up yet. I bailed."

Mac had a glazed-over look in her eyes. I couldn't tell if she was thinking, asleep with her eyes open, or trying not to get sick. "He said lady friend?"

I thought back to what he said. "I don't know, maybe just friend, but woman was implied, I think. I don't remember. Admittedly, I was lost in the gold specs in his eyes."

A smile graced Mac's face, a good sign! "What's his name?"

I shrugged. "I didn't get it. We agreed to stay strangers. I was calling him Mr.

Chardonnay since that was the section of grapes that I sent him down to get to the Love at the Vineyard party."

Mac nodded, pushed away from the table and came to stand beside me. "I love you, but you smell."

"I love you too, and I know. Go back to the party and flirt with your handsome stranger.

Have some fun for one of us. I shall live vicariously through you."

whiny.

"What if I go back and there's a woman there with him?" I said, hating that I sounded

"I have a good feeling. Sometimes when you know, you know. Now go!" "You're an odd duck, Mac."

"Yes, I am but you love me anyway. Go party, I have to go find my Valentine's date, the

pillow."

I waited for her to disappear into my spare room, Olive trailing behind her.

6

Chapter Six

Somehow, in the hour that I was gone, the size of the shindig swelled by nearly double. Sure, a few were latecomers from the other party, but people already in attendance must have invited friends.

"Eloisa! Great idea merging the catering. We needed it!" one of the servers said as I pulled up in the golf cart.

"Where did all these people come from?" I asked, seeing another few cars pulling in. "Social media. Mac was right when she said it was the key to these events. You know

how she loves her hashtags and location tracking. A couple people posted, and more showed up. Apparently, it's the singles event of the year. Congrats!"

She disappeared into the tent, and I was left scratching my head. "Social media baffles me, but damn if I don't love it tonight."

I strolled past one of the vineyard's assistants who were taking and selling tickets to the newcomers. "How's it going? Need help?"

She smiled. "No, I'm good but you should check in with the MC. He was looking for you earlier."

"Okay, thanks. How many new tickets anyway?"

"We're at about fifty, I think. I can count when I get this group in. It's taking a while because we're collecting emails for the newsletter as well as social accounts so we can follow the tags. Mac had these cards made up so people knew what to post."

"She's a genius." I needed to give her a raise.

As I looked around, the first thing I noticed wasn't the amount of people but the age range. "My demo is here."

Mac did it, she got my under forty crowd here! She deserved the best spa day for this

feat.

I said goodbye and peeked into the main section of the gathering space. People milled

about, chatting – all with hands filled with glasses of wine or food. I wished Mac were here to see this. I snapped a couple pictures to text her.

"Hey," someone said beside me. "I was looking for you."

Slowly, I lowered my phone and smiled. Was I hoping it was Mr. Chardonnay? Absolutely, so you could've imagined my disappointment when it was the Master of Ceremonies.

"You found me!" I said in mock-excitement. This guy was *not* my favorite person in the world, but he was great for these events. He was the sort of guy who thought he was funnier than he actually was. But this corny quality played well on stage, and he was one of our more popular MCs.

"I'm getting ready to start another game, but we have a

problem. We have an odd number of participants. You need to step in."

I guffawed. "That'll be a hard no. Thank you and good night. I'll have one of the employees or servers do it."

"Oh, come on. It'll be fun! Besides, they're all busy and you're just standing here," he insisted, grabbing my hand and pulling me into the center of the floor.

"Okay party people, here are the rules. At the beginning of the night, you filled out a five-question survey and we used those answers to come up with a human scavenger hunt. But instead of finding a thing, you're looking for people.

"Here are the five questions: 1) Find someone who likes the same kind of wine you like.

Find someone whose first name initial is the same as yours. 3) Find someone who has the same amount of siblings as you. 4) Find someone whose favorite food is the same as yours. 5) Find someone whose favorite movie is the same as yours.

"Now, When I say go, the first person to find people matching all five questions wins a prize pack from Giordano's Cellars. Remember, you can talk about anything, to each person you meet. Get to know each other while playing this game. Maybe you'll find your perfect match!"

"This is so confusing, what the hell. Why do I need to participate in this? I don't need a prize pack from Giordano's Cellars. I am Giordano's Cellars!" I griped. He just rolled his eyes and walked away, but I tore off after him.

"Hey, hey and another thing. I didn't fill anything out. What the hell am I supposed to do? Take someone else's random answers?"

"Eloisa, read the slip and for once, will you relax?" he said, smiling and plucking the slip from his assistant's hand.

Ello, calm down. I pulled a couple strings from my death bed.

Live a little.

Find someone who likes the same kind of wine you like – Chardonnay ;)

Find someone whose first name initial is the same as yours – Duh

Find someone who has the same amount of siblings as you – I should've counted Olive as your sibling but alas I put you down as an only child.

Find someone whose favorite food is the same as yours – Risotto

Find someone whose favorite movie is the same as yours. – The Goonies

XO

Mac

"You sly bitch," I mumbled under my breath. Of course she knew all my answers. The assistant laughed and walked away. I shot off a text to Mac.

I'll get you for this. Followed by a gif of the Wicked Witch taunting Dorothy.

7

Chapter Seven

Turned out, the MC's ice breaker game was a great way for people who were previously chatting with each other to find new topics to talk about, or chat up other people they hadn't met yet. Okay, maybe he wasn't so bad.

I wandered around, sipping my Moscato and trying to eavesdrop on conversations. I didn't quite know how to go up to someone and ask them if they liked "The Goonies." Plus I didn't want to break into anyone's existing conversation for fear of interrupting a romantic moment.

What I did do was my best in not looking for Mr. Chardonnay. I couldn't, dare I say, wouldn't seek him out. If we happened to bump into each other again, it was fate. But my Grinchly soul wasn't ready to hunt down a hot guy at a Valentine's Day party just yet.

In the end, I didn't have to. He found me hiding in a corner, trying to actively avoid using this damn paper. "You're back," he said, smiling when he ventured over.

"I am," I said simply. "I just couldn't stay away." "I'm glad," he whispered.

"Excuse me?" I said, unsure if that was really what he had said.

"Nothing, just making conversation. How's everything at the other event?"

I didn't know how to explain that it had rapidly devolved into an outright bone-fest, so I just said, "I'll give you one guess. Look at all these people here. They include the last handful of guests from the other event..."

"Well that's a success then, right? This party is huge, and doesn't it still benefit the vineyard?"

I looked up at him and saw that he was asking me a sincere question, and I realized how much I liked his optimism. About the party, about Valentine's Day, and didn't he say he was a hopeless romantic?

"You know what, you're right. It is a success. I should've realized from the start that all people really want is to drink wine and get plowed, and ultimately that's what I brought them tonight. And that, Mr. Chardonnay, is a beautiful thing."

He barked a laugh. An all out full belly laugh. Not only did it light up his face, but he had me laughing as well. At him. At myself. And then it became a vicious cycle of laughter. By the time tears were streaming down my face I forgot what we were laughing about.

"I didn't mean to laugh. I just didn't expect you to be so forthcoming. It's refreshing." "What is? Brutal honesty? You should get out more."

Before he could respond a woman with long red hair

saddled up to him and asked in her most alluring voice, "What's your favorite wine? Mine's Cabernet." And with that, she took a sip. I had to hand it to her, she had seduction down to a T. But just as jealousy started to rear its ugly head, Mr. Chardonnay surprised me with his answer.

"Sorry looks like we're not a match," he winced for her sake. "Mine's Chardonnay," he said and snuck me a wink.

A wink! At me!

She saw it and made a face. "Okay well maybe you'll change your mind." And with that she was gone.

I couldn't help but laugh. "Well that was fun. Maybe this scavenger hunt was a good idea. So is Chardonnay really your favorite wine?" I looked at him skeptically because I'd been around wine drinkers all my life and he did not strike me as a Chardonnay lover.

His shoulder bumped mine. "You caught me. It's Cabernet, but I didn't want to admit that to her."

Just then a man came stumbling over toward me to ask if we were a match. "My friend, the only thing I'm matching you with tonight is an Uber to take you safely home. Excuse me a second," I apologized and took off toward the front room that was blocked from guests.

When I returned, Chardonnay was in the same spot but turned to admire a painting that hung on the wall.

"It's the town my father is from in Italy," I explained by way of announcing my return. "It looks lovely, and hilly. I bet that's a hell of a bike workout. What's it called?" "Scheggia e Pascelupo."

"Wow, I'm not even going to try and pronounce that. Have you been?

I nodded. "Every summer for a couple weeks at a time." I paused, feeling the lump well up. "After my mom left, we skipped a couple years but then we started venturing back. Those summers were some of my favorites."

"Is that why the art is so prominently displayed?"

I looked around the expanse of the crowded room. "Yeah, I guess so. I never really thought about it before. It used to hang in the dining room – that's the room through those French doors, but I moved it here after my dad retired which is—"

I kept staring at the image of the town when I felt him touch my elbow. "Are you still with me? You sort of zoned out there."

I shook my head. "Sorry, I was just going to say it was one of the few things I actually relocated in this building before I just stopped coming in here."

"Explain – if you're willing to talk about it," he said, and his lack of pushing was refreshing.

I frowned. "That building we were in earlier? That's my preferred work space, not here. A lot of the offices are in here but this was our house when we were still a functioning family of three. Once she left, it never felt like a home anymore. Dad made it the offices, and I sought refuge in the old barn space where my Nonno used to work."

I waited for the judgey comments that I usually got, or the quips that Mac lobbed but it didn't come. Imagine my surprise when he said, "Wow, that makes total sense. For what it's worth, the barn seems awesome. Very hipster chic."

I teasingly punched his arm.

"Who knows, maybe all the fun you had tonight will erase

a couple of those bad memories. You might even find Mr. Right here tonight."

I glanced around the room. "Oh, maybe. Lots of options tonight. Let me know if you see anyone I might like."

He narrowed his eyes and I couldn't help but laugh.

I smiled. "Thanks, Chardonnay. Even though that was magnificently cheesy, I needed the

laugh."

"You know, my real name is Alex, so you don't have to keep calling me that."

"Oh man, that stinks." "What? Why?"

"Our first initials don't match. Shame, with that and the fact that we have different favorite wines—mine is Chardonnay," it was my turn to wink, "it looks like we weren't meant to be."

His thickly lashed brown eyes held a smolder, an undeniable yearning. Suddenly my chest felt warm, tight and the pressure was suffocating. I'd never felt this level of intensity within just a few hours of meeting someone. I was heading down a confusing path.

"Well I don't know about that. We still have siblings, favorite food and favorite movie.

I'll start. I have two younger sisters that I am wildly proud of – one is about to defend her dissertation and the other just passed the New York Bar Exam. They're both profoundly smarter than me, what about you?"

My lips formed into a straight line and shook my head. "Nope sorry. I'm an only child."

He dropped his head in mock defeat. One of the servers

came around with a fiery cheese from a local farmer, and our smoky Pinot Noir. "Try this, it's got a kick if you like spice, but the wine balances it out nicely."

"Don't think I don't know that you're changing the subject," he said. "Is the conversation getting too personal?"

"I have no idea what you're talking about. Put the cheese in your mouth."

"Feisty." He raised an eyebrow and took the samples. "This is so good. A couple times tonight, I've had really great food and wine pairings. I'm impressed by the thought that went into this whole thing."

Mr. Chardonnay's hand was just about to touch mine. Well, I thought it was. We set the glasses down, our eyes were locked, and his fingers flexed against the baby pink tablecloth.

My focus was split between that wily index finger, and the way the candlelight danced in his eyes. The server came back over, and I glared. So much so that I scared her, and she took off in the other direction.

"What are you thinking about so hard? I feel like I can see all the gears moving," he asked, moving his hand closer to mine.

I inhaled sharply when his pinky touched mine. A god damned pinky practically sent me into his arms. I needed help, or more wine. Whichever came first.

"I'm thinking that I've known you for three hours, and that scares me."

"What scares you? The timeframe or the fact that we seem like we like each other after a short amount of time?"

"The second one. And you like me?" I said, smiling and wrapping my pinky finger around

his.

"I dare say I do. And I get being hung up on the time. You're not the only one

questioning if you could really like someone this much after a couple hours but maybe when you know, you know."

Déjà vu hits me like a ton of bricks. "What did you say?"

"When you know, you know?"

I laughed. "Yeah, it's just that's the second time I heard that tonight. My friend Mac said it earlier."

Slowly he pulled his hand away and backed up from the table. He looked at me as if he was seeing me for the first time again.

"I should've seen this. I mean you own the vineyard so of course you'd know Mac." "Wait you know Mac?" I was confused by this whole interaction now.

"Yeah, I was supposed to meet her here."

8

Chapter Eight

"Alex, the pharmacist? You're Alex. The pharmacist," I sputtered as all the times Mac would try to talk about her dear friend Alex, the one she'd been trying to set me up with for ages, flash through my mind. At my outburst, a woman walking by paused when she heard the word pharmacist.

"Oh, you're cute and a doctor? Are you single?"

He turned, annoyed. "Pharmacists aren't medical doctors. I just have a doctorate in Pharmacy."

"Lame." She flipped her hair and left.

Alex, Mr. Chardonnay, turned back to me, and I wanted to ask him so many questions but how many of them did I already know the answers to. "Mac's been trying to fix me up for ages with her friend Alex, the pharmacist. I kept blowing her off because blind dates, yuck!" I mock gagged, before wondering something. "Did you know who I was from the beginning?"

Alex tossed his hands in the air. "I had no idea, I swear."

"Mac!" we both shouted at once and reached for our phones presumably to call her. "Voicemail," he said.

"Same. She's probably asleep—she's at my house. I'm going to kill her if she's not already dead."

"Mac insisted I come tonight specifically to meet someone, but she wouldn't tell me

who."

"I can't believe her but seriously you're not at all what I picture when I think

pharmacist."

He laughed. "What do you think of when you think of a pharmacist?

"Solid point, and I think pocket protector, thick glasses and bald, like they show you in the wee-hours of the morning commercials for erection pills."

His lips curled in as he tried not to laugh. "I honestly wonder where you come up with some of this."

"If you find the answer, let me know. Mac and I have been trying to figure it out for years. Seriously though, why did you come?"

He smiled and shrugged. "I didn't have anything else to do so I figured why not? My last relationship ended about a year ago and since then I'm either working or golfing, when possible. Winter in upstate New York doesn't exactly allow the latter all that often so I read, a lot. But tonight, what better day to get back on the metaphorical horse than Valentine's Day.

She sent me a ticket and told me what time to be here. I knew I was at the wrong event earlier, but I was trying to find

Mac and then you were there. I didn't find out about the food poisoning until right before you got back to this event—but I didn't realize you were the person she wanted me to meet."

"I should have introduced myself from the beginning. I'm Eloisa. Did she tell you my name?"

Alex shook his head.

"Mac could've saved us a lot of confusion."

"I wouldn't change a thing. We were honest when we thought each other were strangers."

"You're right. Still though—if I had known it was you—"

"Don't finish that. I have a feeling you would've purposefully avoided me," he said as he laughed.

"That's because I—Christ, I don't know why. I could kick myself now. She was right to want to introduce us," I slapped a hand over my mouth. "Don't repeat that, I'll deny it. I can't let her think she was right."

His head fell back with a peel of laughter. "I promise, Eloisa." "Ello. My friends, they call me Ello."

"Now what?" he asked, rolling up the sleeves a bit higher allowing me to study his arm.

I could see a bit more of the tattoo now. It was ornate, and while I didn't know what all of it was, I could see one specific part that made me smile.

"Alex, we still have questions left to answer and they're important." "Okay…"

"My favorite food is risotto, what is yours?" He broke into a huge smile when he realized where I was going with this.

"I'm sorry to say, it's steak."

"We're 0 for 4! It all comes down to the final question—

may I?" I asked, reaching out to touch his arm. I waited for him to nod before I unbuttoned the cuff and rolled the sleeve as far up as it would go.

"I've been admiring this all night but I couldn't see it until now." "Are you anti-tattoo?"

I bit my lip. "Not at all. I have ten actually, but I have one more question for you." "Shoot," he said, pushing in a bit closer to close the gap between us. His arm was

awkwardly sandwiched between us but somehow, it felt perfect here.

Maybe things really did happen for a reason.

I was supposed to run into him. We were meant to talk about our lives with no preconceived notions and we perhaps, were meant to be each other's plus one with this party game.

"What is the best movie that all children must watch?" Alex chuckled. "Are you kidding me?"

"Nope, you have to answer it."

"The answers to that question and what my favorite movie is are the same. The Goonies."

I shake my head in amusement. "I can't believe it. That is my all-time favorite movie and has been since I was a kid."

"How'd you know? Can I ask what gave it away?"

"The tattoo. I couldn't see it before and when I finally did, I noticed you had one that said, 'Never Say Die' and I knew that as long as we have that one thing in common, we'd be okay."

We both stared at his ornately designed tattoo and when I looked up, he was staring at me so intently it was like he could feel what I felt, see what I saw. He leaned in towards me, tilting his head slightly, and kissed me. In that second, every nerve in my body exploded and I knew that this event, this Valentine's Day, would be one I'd always remember.

Epilogue

"Where are we headed?" Alex asked, giving my hand a small squeeze.

"Listen, Mr. Impatient, I said it was a surprise. That means, you wait until we get there and no peeking."

I let go of his hand and stood in front of him. Looking at the scarf I tied around his eyes, I hoped that he really couldn't see out of it like he insisted earlier.

"What are you doing?" he asked, as I was untucking my shirt.

I gripped the hem of my Henley and pulled it up over my head. For good measure, I did a little jiggle. No reaction.

"Nothing, just a little test."

He shrugged. "Are we there yet?"

"Good lord, you're like a toddler in the backseat headed for vacation. Relax!"

I led him deeper into the vineyard, staying between the vines but heading far enough off the main path that we wouldn't be seen.

"Okay, here. You can remove the scarf."

"If I leave it on, will you show me your boobs again?"

I punched his arm. "You shit! You said you couldn't see through the scarf!"

He pulled the scarf down. "They were blurry but I can recognize your boobs. Besides, can you blame me?"

I thought about it. "Maybe later you'll see more boobs, but for now, snacks."

He set up the blankets, and I got to work on the makeshift charcuterie board with delightful salted meats, and creamy cheeses and of course, wine.

"To what do I owe this special treat?" Alex asked and handed me the corkscrew. "You really don't know what today is?" I teased, jutting my bottom lip out playfully.

He looked perplexed, rightfully so as today wasn't anything special. I was just messing with him.

"It can't be our three month anniversary because that was last week," he said. "Aw, you're tracking our monthly anniversaries? That's sweet, Mr. Romance." "Don't tell me you're not doing the same thing, Miss Closet Romantic."

"I have no idea what you're talking about." I booped him on the nose. "Wait, then what's so special about today?"

I shrugged. "I was just kidding, though it seems worth celebrating that today is the first nice, really warm day of May. No rain, the sun is shining and we both had a free afternoon, so I thought, let's get tipsy in the sunshine and see what happens."

He leaned forward capturing my lips in a searing kiss. "I have a pretty good idea what's going to happen, and it involves that scarf and that sturdy looking post behind you."

"Sounds like someone has a wild imagination."

He leaned in and pressed his lips to mine. "You're about to find out."

About the Author

Nina Bocci is a USA Today Bestselling novelist, publicist, eternal optimist, unabashed lipgloss enthusiast, constanta-pologist and a hopeless romanticist. She has too many college degrees that she's not using and a Lego addiction that she blames on her son. You can contact

Nina via her website https://ninabocci. com/